CW00252876

The Secret Diary of a Professional Grasscutter

By Katherine Robson

HELEN NEWMAN WOOD

Copyright © 2024 Helen Newman Wood

The right of Helen Newman Wood to be identified as the author of
this work has been asserted to them in accordance with the
Copyright, Design and Patents Act 1988.

Cover photograph Copyright © 2024 Helen Newman Wood

All rights reserved.

This work is entirely fictitious and bears no resemblance to any
persons living or dead.

For Ian, Gail, and Professional Grasscutters everywhere

A SUMMER JOB

This happened because Pirate-Pete sold the Newsagent's and moved to Magaluf.

I was a bit shocked to start with because I'd worked in *Pete's Papers* since I was fourteen, and I couldn't really picture Pete working on a door in The Magaluf Strip. He told me they weren't called 'Bouncers' anymore, he said he was moving to Majorca to be a 'Clientele Control Operative'.

Whatever.

Some people said that Pirate-Pete was a grumpy so-and-so, but I always got on alright with him. He used to give me out of date crisps when he gave me my wages and I didn't even notice his false leg and eye patch after a while.

The people who bought the Newsagent's said they didn't need me anymore, because they had a sixteen-year-old son who wanted to do the paper round and help in the shop. I didn't think this was that much of a deal. After all, I'm starting college in September, but mum kept banging on and on about me getting a job for the summer. Then Dad said Uncle Dave kept moaning that there weren't enough hours in the day to cut all the lawns he had been contracted to do.

And I mean it can't be hard, can it? Walking behind a lawnmower for a couple of days a week, surely can't be that hard? Uncle Dave is nearly fifty and he manages to do it five days a week and he smokes forty Lambert & Butler Blues a day. And when I say he likes a beer, this can be roughly translated as: *goes to the pub on a Friday night and re-emerges on a Monday morning.*

So I agreed to this grass cutting thing after Uncle Dave agrees (begrudgingly), to pay me £15 an hour and to buy me lunch every fourth Friday. He says it'll be nice to spend some time with his only niece, but I know this is bollocks because he's told me to bring something to read at lunchtimes. I'm not stupid. I know this is so I can look after the van (the driver's door doesn't lock and neither do the back doors and

Uncle Dave says his Honda lawnmowers are worth a fortune), while he nips off for a quick pint of Carling at whichever pub we're nearest to.

And this is how I have found myself travelling around the coastal villages of Northumberland, in a battered Citroen Berlingo van that smells of petrol, fag ends and wet dog.

TUESDAY 6TH JULY

I have to meet Uncle Dave at the little holiday cottages on the dunes.

It's nine o' clock and as it's already pretty warm, I put my hoodie and rucksack on top of a wheelie bin while I wait for Uncle Dave and when he does finally appear, I can't tell if his van is belching black smoke from the exhaust or if it's just fag smoke from the driver's window.

Find my bloody hoodie has slipped off the wheelie bin and landed in some weird-looking thistle-like plant on the ground. I pick it up and start trying to pull the spikey bits off the fabric, only to find that the thistle things are literally disintegrating in my fingers and leaving massive spikes in my favourite blue hoodie.

Uncle Dave is out of the van like a shot. I mean, I had no idea he could even move that fast, it was like last orders had been called at the *Happy Frog* on a Friday night. He takes my hoodie off me like it's contaminated and puts it in a carrier bag he's got out the back of his van.

'Pirri Pirri Bur,' he advises, the ash falling off the end of his Lambert & Butler as he securely knots the plastic handles of the bag. 'I'll burn it later.'

I start to protest, but realise I've lost my audience because Uncle Dave is now explaining that the land here is very sandy, the grass is poor, and therefore I shouldn't cut the lawns too low.

I have no clue what he means and after he's manhandled a lawnmower out of his van and shown me how to start it, I just crack on and start my first lawn, while Uncle Dave pours weedkiller onto the Pirri Pirri thing.

After cutting half the lawn, I notice that the bit I've cut is practically bare earth. I quickly Google the model of the lawnmower on my phone and add 'cutting the grass low' into the search bar. For being a popular tourist place the signal on my phone is bloody useless and the page takes ages to load.

I discover the mower has these notch things beside the wheels which makes the blade kind of go up and down. Ah! I raise the deck (Did you spot that? I've got the terminology already and it's not even ten o' clock) and find the rest of the lawn looks like I've cut the grass and not scraped the turf away with a JCB bucket.

It's seventeen degrees and sweat is pissing down my forehead and my jeans are sticking to my arse. I think of asking Uncle Dave if I can nip home and change but think better of it when I see him wielding the strimmer like an Olympic discus thrower.

We have a lot of lawns to cut today as it's meant to rain for the next two days. If the predicted thunderstorms arrive tomorrow morning, I get an unplanned day off, so I could go to the Metrocentre and buy a new shirt for going to the pub on Friday night. Or I could just spend the day surfing the internet trying to find those trousers with the zip-off legs and some more appropriate footwear than my white trainers, which are already turning green.

At some point in the morning, Uncle Dave announces that it's coffee time and pauses for thirty seconds to down half a cup of stewed Nescafé from his flask and eat a Kit Kat, before donning his goggles again and starting the strimmer.

For God's sake.

I drink half a can of Coke and then do battle with the sparse grass under a washing line on a hill that is so steep, the perfect person to mow it successfully would be a three-foot tall rock climber. Finally disentangle myself from an XL size pair of Y-fronts, several beige socks and a bra that would be too big for Dolly Parton, and move on to my next victim.

This one is easier because the lawn is flat, but it's surrounded by various scratchy shrubs that are all at elbow height. Make mental note to wear long sleeves tomorrow and to Google 'Pirri Pirri Burr' to find out why my hoodie has been condemned to death.

At quarter-past-three, the first raindrops start to land. Judging by the black clouds rolling in from the sea, I've got a day off tomorrow.

FRIDAY 9TH JULY

So, according to Google, Pirri Pirri is a plant native to New Zealand and Australia, and it probably came to Northumberland on the fleeces of imported sheep. It's known as Bidgee-widgee in its native land, and the seeds that washed off the coats of the sheep imported to the docks at Berwick upon Tweed in the early 1900's, then made their way to the island of Lindisfarne, where it's now causing a big problem. The burrs stick to animals, shoelaces, clothing, in fact anything; and therefore, spread rapidly. Hence Uncle Dave burning my hoodie in a metal dustbin at his lock-up last night with a manic grin on his face. The sad thing, is that bird watchers on Lindisfarne have spotted migrant Thrushes so covered in Pirri Pirri Weed that they are unable to fly.

Anyway, after a night of Googling this bizarre plant, I'm knackered before I even meet Uncle Dave at Aidan Drive in the village of Cresthill.

Thankfully, I packed my work bag last night before I started Googling Pirri Pirri Weed and today I'm armed with shorts (in case it gets hot), one of Dad's brushed cotton shirts (in case of more evil, pointy bushes that have left cuts on my arms as if I self-harm), extra sandwiches (was starving on my first day), three cans of Monster (see last point), and a litre of water (by four o' clock on Tuesday I could have licked a sweaty tourist).

I start cutting the grass in Number Eighteen, a holiday house that is so big, five families could live in it and not bump into each other. I've only done one lap of the back lawn when an upstairs window opens, and an angry man asks me if I know what time it is? He seems even crosser when I reply that it's seven-minutes-past-nine and he swears a lot and tells me to go away and come back later.

I go to the holiday home next door. I might be okay here as there are no cars on the drive, but my mower refuses to start. I drag Uncle Dave away from his whirlwind strimmer action and he informs me that the mower won't start unless it's cold or hot. It doesn't like being tepid. Stupid thing. After five minutes I'm off again and make short work of Number Twenty.

Uncle Dave points out that my mowed lines aren't straight. I ask him if he wants the bloody grass cut or not? He suggests I lower the mower and do it again.

I've done Number Twenty-Two by the time Uncle Dave announces that it's coffee time. He fills the cup from his Thermos with coffee, downs it, shovels in a Double Decker and he's off again. I put my half-empty can of Coke in the cup holder in the front of the van. On Tuesday I left it on the pavement and got a fizzing mouthful of four caffeine-infused, drowning wasps when I went to finish it at lunchtime.

Uncle Dave stops strimming for a nanosecond to gesticulate towards Number Twenty-Four.

I push my mower towards it and mow the tiny lawn in front of the house. I have to wrestle open the fence-panel gate and beyond the greenhouse on the patio, I find the sadistic bastards who live here, have *occasional* flowerbeds scattered across their back lawn. It's like trying to manoeuvre a shopping trolley with a wonky wheel around an army assault course.

I *accidentally* shred a Hosta and a clump of Lady's Mantle.

As it's Friday, Uncle Dave declares that he will get us lunch. I suggest the nice catering van along the road that serves Lobster rolls and Monkfish skewers. Uncle Dave chokes and has a massive coughing fit as he lights a Lambert & Butler, telling me to go back to Number Eighteen and he'll be back with food by the time I've finished.

No cars outside sweary-angry man's holiday house now, so I get to work on the back lawn. Luckily, they've left some towels on the washing line and I use them to wipe the petrol off my hands after refuelling the mower.

Uncle Dave returns with a cold scotch pie, a packet of pickled onion Space Raiders, a Freddo Frog, and a can of Iron-Bru.

Can't help but feel cheated.

TUESDAY 13TH JULY

Meet Uncle Dave in Ebba Road which is mostly old people living in big houses.

This is better. By eleven-thirty-four I've been offered four coffees, a bacon roll, six biscuits, and three glasses of juice.

I like the old Major, who lives in the house called Island View. He's got a proper handlebar moustache and offers me a can of Boddingtons and a bottle of Speckled Hen, the minute I push the mower into his garden.

As I mow around a Churchill Mk IV Tank, I notice there's a faint smell of cat pee coming from the garden next door.

Uncle Dave appears and drinks the Boddingtons and the Speckled Hen while I finish the lawn in front of the Major's Conservatory. He tells me to start Mrs Higginsbottom's back garden next door and he will do the front garden. He adds that if I am ever offered cake on this street, I must always refuse it, and only take biscuits that come from Aldi or Sainsbury's. God, it's like I'm seven years old. He'll be telling me not to go off with strangers to look at puppies next.

Mrs Higginsbottom is sitting on her patio listening to the radio. She offers me a coffee and tells me to only cut the grass as far as the hedge that stretches across her garden, because she leaves the bottom of her garden around her greenhouses, as a wild area for the bees and butterflies.

I must be coming down with something. I feel slightly woozy when I finish her lawn and start craving crisps and sweets.

Pushing the mower along the pavement to Highgates, I pass two kids with their faces painted with cat's whiskers. I make a clawing gesture and yell a loud 'Meow!' then get the giggles and can't stop laughing.

Trying to stop sniggering, I begin the lawn at Highgates, where the nice old lady introduces herself as 'Elvis' and hands me a bag of Haribo. Manage to eat half the bag and avoid all the green gummy bears, while Elvis sits on her decking with her headphones on.

I've finished the lawn before I realise my trainers look like those huge fluffy slippers you can buy on the internet, and Uncle Dave points out that I haven't had the catcher box on the mower, making Elvis's lawn look like it's been cut for sileage. I tell Elvis I'm sorry and that I'll cut it again to collect all the clippings, but she just says: 'It's cool, man' and I slip away as she starts opening a family-sized bag of Walker's Sensations.

THURSDAY 15TH JULY

I've lost 5lb.

I think it's probably just fluid as I'm sweating so much behind this bloody mower but still, 5lb is not to be sneezed at.

We're back at the cottages on the dunes and as we haven't had as much rain as predicted, the grass hasn't grown much. Great. So there's no need to be emptying the catcher box like a mad woman with OCD on amphetamines today.

Manage to get Uncle Dave to deal with the climbing wall with the washing line on it, and notice that the same underpants, bra, and socks are pegged out as they were two weeks ago.

I ask Uncle Dave if the people who live here are OK. I mean, they could be dead if their washing has been out for that long. Uncle Dave says the washing has been hanging on the line for years as the bank is too steep for the old couple to retrieve their smalls.

I unpeg it all, fold it, and leave their laundry, along with the rusty pegs, on the back doorstep.

After lunch it's back up to Ebba Road.

The Major is fast asleep in a deckchair right in the middle of his lawn. He doesn't stir as I cut the grass and it's only when I bump the ice bucket containing four bottles of Abbot Reserve, that he mutters something in his sleep and pulls his Panama hat lower over his face.

I leave him there, on a rectangle of grass that's half an inch longer than the rest of his lawn.

Mrs Higginsbottom is out but has left five cans of Coke in a cool box and a Tupperware container containing a number of cakes, with a note telling me to help myself but not to eat more than two. The chocolate fudge cake is gorgeous but after I've eaten a slice of ginger cake, I just want to sit and watch her Laburnum tree swaying gently in the breeze. Wow. I mean, just *wow*. It's beautiful and I want to live in this moment forever.

I wake up to Uncle Dave slapping my face and shouting, 'Oh for f**k's sake, NEVER touch the cakes!!!'

Uncle Dave says I've done enough for today and takes me home. I find an out-of-date packet of Salt and Vinegar Discos in the glove box and finish them off with a multipack of Crunchies that Uncle Dave had tucked behind the driver's seat.

FRIDAY 16TH JULY

As the grass is growing faster than Jeremy Clarkson's farming fan club, Uncle Dave has asked me to do an extra day this week.

He finished Mrs Higginsbottom's yesterday so I start at Highgates, where Elvis is holding some kind of Tai-Chi in her back garden. Well, at first I thought it looked like Tai-Chi but after I'm halfway through cutting the lawn, it looks like they're just dancing to 'All Shook Up' really slowly. Like, really, really, slowly.

I spot an empty Tupperware box on the patio and lots of unfinished cake on tea plates on the patio table.

After lunch it's back to Aidan Drive. Most of the holiday houses are empty as it's changeover day, but there's one family having a barbeque in their back garden. I eat a burger, two lamb kebabs, a piece of corn on the cob and two chicken legs and then find the mower hard to manage as the handlebar part is all greasy.

I nip up to Number Twenty-Four and find a mesh fence has been erected around the Hosta I decimated last week.

Accidentally run over their Hoselock sprinkler system.

TUESDAY 20TH JULY

To celebrate losing another 2lb, I start the day by pushing copper nails into the Weeping Willow in the back garden of Number Ten on Aidan Drive. It's an utter bastard to cut around and last week when I got in the shower after work, I found half of it stuck in my hair.

I've found some tree poison on Ebay, but this will only stop the tree from growing back after you've cut it down. This might only be a holiday house, but I'm fairly certain the cleaning team who come here will notice that I've taken a chainsaw to the sodding Willow. Make a mental note to ask Uncle Dave if there are any diseases that attack Weeping Willows.

Mid-afternoon, we head back to the cottages on the dunes to do the three we didn't have time to do last week. The enormous pants, beige socks and oversized bra are back on the line and there's a laminated sign on the washing line prop that says:

Thank you for bringing our washing in but I leave it out so people think we're at home. We do not want to get burgled again

I Google 'security alarms' and write the website addresses I find, on the laminated sheet with a green permanent marker pen I found in the door pocket of Uncle Dave's van.

The people staying in the big holiday house opposite the washing line, have a cockerpoo, a German Shepherd, a Great Dane, and a Golden retriever with them. They assure me they have cleared the lawns of all dog shit and in my naivety, I actually believe them. That is, until I run over a pile so big it should have had its own what3words reference, and it's everywhere. Splattered over my shins and trainers and the smell makes me retch.

I don't empty the catcher box until the mower is spewing

grass clippings like a vomiting toddler, and I try not to touch the box as I tip the clippings into the compost bin. Notice three tennis balls, a rubber chew and a raggy piece of rope and manage to mulch the lot of them with my mower. Pretend to be deaf when the lady starts asking the Cockerpoo what he's done with his favourite toys.

FRIDAY 23RD JULY

It's Friday, and Uncle Dave comes back at lunchtime smelling strongly of Carling and brandishing a steak and onion pie. When I ask him if he's not hungry he replies: 'I had a quick toastie at the pu—' then coughs and says he's not feeling well.

In sheer defiance, once we start on Ebba Road, I accept the can of Boddington's from the Major and a pint of vodka and tonic from Mrs Higginsbottom, but I tell her I'm not hungry when she offers me cake. She looks mightily disappointed and mutters something about 'a waste of 25% THC'. By the time I've cut her lawn I'm desperate for a massive bag of Twiglets and a Twirl.

No sign of Elvis today, just a two-tone bowling shirt and a pair of penny loafers by the side of the chair where she/he/Elvis usually sits. It's only when I'm finished and am pushing the mower across the gravel at the front of the house, that I notice a bucket full of cold water and five cans of Coke bobbing about in it. Bless her. Bless him. Bless Elvis.

Late afternoon, we nip back to the houses on the dunes and I do the lawn next door to the holiday house with the Cockerpoo, German Shepherd, Great Dane, and Golden Retriever.

I'm shocked at how satisfied I feel when I hear the lady telling Raymond-the-Cockerpoo that he needs to be more careful with his toys as they all seem to have disappeared. I cross my fingers and hope she doesn't check the compost heap and see evidence of the shredding.

To be fair, if she does, it will smell strongly of dog shit.

TUESDAY 27TH JULY

Uncle Dave has a new house on his list, and he drops me and my mower off at the front gate assuring me he'll be back in a while, after he's cut another new property he has on his list.

I merrily cut the two pieces of grass in front of the sliding glass frontage and am whistling a tune as I drag the mower to the back of the house. The sun is shining, I'm wearing my shorts, my shoulders are tanning and life could be worse.

However, it turns out, Uncle Dave knew what he was doing here. The lawn is on a 45-degree angle, the size of St James' Park, and the water feature with two cherubs spitting water into a clam shell is leaking. I almost sprain my ankle trying to avoid the boggy part around the fountain and don't speak to Uncle Dave when he grins and asks if I managed it okay.

Uncle Dave knows I'm in the huff and this is definitely why he suggests a quick pint at the Happy Frog once we've finished for the day. To drum home my point, instead of asking for my usual pint of *Sheep Leghumper*, I ask for a *Twim Peake* cocktail. This is nine different spirits, poured in layers and served with whipped cream, sugar stars, a sparkler, a chocolate Hobnob and a shot of Rainbow Sourz.

I'm just finishing it when Mrs Higginsbottom comes in. She says she does love a *Twim Peake* but can't have more than two. She orders an *Irish Slammer*, and I watch in astonishment as she drops a shot of whisky and a shot of Baileys into half a pint of Guinness, drinks it in one motion and then slaps her thighs and says: 'onwards and upwards!' and leaves.

Uncle Dave has finished his pint of Carling but when I suggest another, he coughs and says we should be getting home.

Miserable git.

THURSDAY 29TH JULY

I think there's something wrong with Elvis.

She's/He's/Elvis is lying on a sunlounger on the patio, wearing a white suit, dark glasses, penny loafers and a Stetson. I cut the whole lawn and Elvis doesn't stir. I even sit on the end of the sunlounger and give the penny loafers a wobble and still Elvis sleeps like a baby.

Uncle Dave appears asking why I've been so long, and he shakes his head as I point at Elvis. He laughs when I say there's something wrong with her/him/Elvis and gestures to the crumb-covered tea plate on the patio table.

I've never known anyone fall asleep after cake. I mean, my dad falls asleep as soon as he's finished his Christmas dinner, but not after eating cake.

Mid-morning, it's back down to do a couple of houses on the dunes and, despite hinting to Uncle Dave that a lobster roll with lemon mayonnaise would be nice, he just grunts and pulls his lunchbox out from behind his seat in the van. He's got egg mayo today and I sit on the verge outside the van to eat my ham roll to avoid the stench.

Uncle Dave has another new house on his list and Mrs Taylor, who owns it, brings us both a cup of coffee as we're finishing our lunch. Uncle Dave rummages around in the door pocket of the van and finds four sugar sticks he's stolen from Macdonald's, but the coffee still tastes a bit strange.

After lunch, which is the shortest hour of the day, I shove open the high garden gate to Mrs Taylor's back garden with my mower, and find I'm face to face with a brown and white goat.

Mrs Taylor calls out that 'Martha' won't hurt me and I'm just to mow around her and would I like some goat's milk to take home with me? That explains the funny-tasting coffee then. I thank her but decline the offer of Martha's milk and crack on with the grass. I'm not amused that Mrs Taylor thinks it's hilarious that Martha follows me around as I pace up and down the garden. Every time I stop to empty the catcher, bloody Martha starts chewing my t-shirt.

Uncle Dave can do this one next week.

TUESDAY 3RD AUGUST

There's a massive party going on in the garden with that bloody Weeping Willow on Aidan drive.

We didn't start work this morning until nearly 10 o' clock, because Uncle Dave had forgotten to buy petrol for the mowers. We had to queue for ages at the garage because there was an ambulance tending to someone in the car that was completely blocking the two petrol pumps.

I was a bit worried because Uncle Dave smoked half a packet of Lambert & Butler while we were waiting for the paramedics to do their stuff. I mean, I was worried that he was going to turn us into a massive fireball, not that he was going to have a heart attack. Stupid old git.

Edna, who lives around the corner from Uncle Dave, had stopped with her pull-along shopping trolley that was clanking with bottles, and told us she thought the driver of the old Mercedes was having a *funny turn*.

Turns out, it was Elvis who had fallen asleep in her/his/Elvis's car while she/he/Elvis was waiting for the car in front to pay for their fuel and drive away. Once Elvis woke up and despite the paramedics suggesting she/he/Elvis should go with them to hospital to be checked over, she/he/Elvis drove off really slowly, with 'Hound Dog' playing really, really loudly.

Uncle Dave says if we get Aidan Drive finished today, we're not doing Elvis's lawn. Well, what he actually said was: 'We're not doing that effing stoner's grass today. We'll end up in an effing coma if we go anywhere near the place.'

Anyway, the party at the Weeping Willow house must have been going on all night as there were ten of them squeezed into the hot tub on the patio. They said they didn't mind at all if I cut the grass and just turned the music up louder.

As I emptied the grass box on the mower, I saw the biggest bloke, who must have been twenty stone, attempting to climb on top of the weeping willow. There was a kind of wailing noise as I pushed the mower to Number Sixteen, and they were still laughing in the hot tub when I went across the road to cut the grass at Number Thirteen.

THURSDAY 5TH AUGUST

Oh my God.

It seems Ebba Road are having some sort of community gathering in the Major's garden. There's a new inflatable hot tub on the patio and a sound system has been set up. Elvis is in the hot tub, fully clothed, and Mrs Higginsbottom is dancing around waving silk scarves in the air like a stoned Air Traffic Controller.

The Major tells me not to worry about the grass and just to come back another time, then he gives me a bottle of Speckled Hen and a can of Waggle Dance and suggests I help myself to a piece of cake or a biscuit from the plate on the wooden table.

After a bit of hesitation, I take a Sainsbury's mini roll and haul my mower across the gravel path as fast as I can.

We nip back to the cottages on the dunes, and I see there's no enormous underwear on the washing line above the tendon-snapping climbing wall and a shiny new alarm system has been installed on the house.

There's no-one in at the holiday house next door but the lawn is covered in dog shit. I mow around each landmine and leave the lawn looking like a drone shot of the Outer Hebrides.

TUESDAY 10TH AUGUST

I start at the Major's on Ebba Road having missed last week owing to his community gathering.

He greets me at the patio door looking seriously unwell and mutters something about *comedown*. Not sure what he means, but after cutting half the lawn he stops me with a two-and-a-half litre bottle of Frosty Jack's Cider. He suggests I just leave the grass until next week because he has a headache so bad, if he opens his eyes properly 'there's a jolly good chance' he'll bleed to death. I ask if I can get him paracetamol and he says: 'No, no. We've had our annual cake and sherry festival, and it always takes one some time to detox.'

No sign of Mrs Higginsbottom, but there's four cans of cat food and a tin of Heinz beans and sausages in the cool box instead of the usual cans of coke.

Elvis greets me with a cheery wave and sits on the patio listening to 'Jailhouse Rock' through the massive sound system that was at the Major's last week. It's a good job they're all Elvis fans on this street. She/he/Elvis offers me a piece of toffee cake and assures me that Mrs Higginsbottom didn't make it, she/he/Elvis bought it herself/himself/their self from the local bakers. It's only when I've eaten half of it, Elvis suddenly remembers that Mrs Higginsbottom iced it.

Eat three packets of Quavers, a Bounty, a Drumstick Lolly, and a packet of Refreshers Squashies that Uncle Dave had stashed in the glove box, on the way home.

THURSDAY 12TH AUGUST

Uncle Dave has pulled a fast one here.

Since I met Martha the goat and mad Mrs Taylor, I've managed to body-swerve doing her grass. Reading between the lines (or so Barry-the-Builder told me in the Happy Frog), Uncle Dave had a terrible experience with Mrs Taylor last week and has been avidly avoiding the houses on the dunes ever since.

From what Barry-the-Builder said, Uncle Dave was so fixated on avoiding mowing down Martha, he didn't notice that Mrs Taylor was sunbathing on her patio completely starkers. He'd cut nearly all the back lawn before Mrs Taylor stood up, and yelled *what did she have to do to get a man to notice her*, then stomped off into the house in a huff. Because Uncle Dave was standing there, gawping at her disappearing rear view like a thirteen-year-old boy finding OnlyFans for the first time, he failed to notice that Martha had almost destroyed the arse of his jeans and had eaten one sleeve of his favourite Oasis t-shirt.

I cut Mrs Taylor's lawns in record time, but in fairness when you have a free-range goat, there's not a lot of grass to cut.

Gaz, who works in the Happy Frog in the evenings, is painting the garden fence a nice shade of mint green, and I notice Mrs Taylor standing behind the patio door brandishing a pair of binoculars. I ask Gaz if he's been working for Mrs Taylor long and he replies that he's painted the fence three times this week, because Mrs Taylor couldn't decide which colour worked best. I look at Gaz's bulging biceps and wonder if Mrs Taylor really needs a Professional Grasscutter.

Late morning, it's up to Aidan Drive but we're rained off by lunchtime. Me and Uncle Dave stop at the Frog for a quick pint which turns into several pints, half a dozen whisky chasers and four jugs of Bramble Ramble.

Clearly the story about Uncle Dave and Mrs Taylor and

Martha is doing the rounds.

Whenever Uncle Dave comes back into the bar from the gents, everyone starts singing 'Row, row, row your goat' and when Barry-the-Builder comes in at half past nine, he calls Uncle Dave *Billy the Kid* and asks him if he's going to grow a *goatee* for Movember.

When Uncle Dave tells him to get stuffed, Barry replies that Uncle Dave shouldn't *butt in* and that he was only *kidding*. Then Barry started singing: 'Who let the goats out, maa, maa, maa, maa' and Uncle Dave said if he didn't stop taking the piss he was going to thump him. Brian, the landlord, had to get involved to stop the fight and, after Barry and Uncle Dave had sat down again at the bar, Brian started singing 'How much is that goatee in the window' and Uncle Dave punched him.

Got barred before last orders.

FRIDAY 13TH AUGUST

Because we got rained off yesterday, Uncle Dave wants to try and catch up today. I've got a blinding hangover and I think Uncle Dave has too, because by ten-thirty he's whimpering like a dying dog and lying in the back of the van which is parked on Aidan Drive.

I cut Number Ten, Number Eighteen and *accidentally* destroy a length of hose and a ceramic pot at Number Twenty-Four.

When I stop for lunch, I discover that Uncle bloody Dave is still fast asleep in the back of the van. I eat my tuna mayo sandwich and then eat Uncle Dave's cheese and pickle roll and his mini pork pie. After a quick search behind the driver's seat, I find a packet of fizzy cola bottles and stuff them in my pocket for later.

I've just started Number Thirteen when the heavens open again, and the rain is running off my chin by the time I get the mower back to the van.

Uncle Dave's still asleep and his feet are sticking out of the van's back doors in the rain. I sit in the passenger seat to eat the bag of cola bottles as the rain pours down the windscreen. I wait until I have used my green index finger to wipe the fizzy sugar out of the bottom of the bag before I wake him.

MONDAY 16TH AUGUST

Because of Uncle Dave's monstrous hangover and the rain last week, we're well behind, and because of the rain, the grass is growing quicker than the queue at a tattoo parlour in Ibiza, at two in the morning.

We start on Aidan Drive, and I head to Ebba Road after lunch, leaving Uncle Dave to do the two properties outside the village; and the forty-five-degree incline that is St James' Park with the dodgy water feature. I know he won't do St James' Park with the puking cherubs. I just know it.

There's a right crowd at Highgates.

They're playing Twister, which (aside from the risk of a broken hip happening at any second) I think is a bit unfair because Mrs Smithson (who used to run the Post Office) is in a wheelchair. It doesn't seem to bother her though, as Elvis just pushes a wheel of her chair onto whatever colour spot she has to be on.

I'm emptying the second box of grass clippings onto Elvis's compost heap when I hear yelling. I shout to ask if everything is OK and Elvis calls back that everything is fine; Mrs Smithson has just run over the Major's hand.

I ask if he needs a cold compress, but Elvis replies that he would be better with a piece of Lemon Drizzle cake.

Once I've finished the lawn and then been called to judge if Mrs Higginsbottom has indeed got her left hand on green, her right foot on red, and her right elbow on yellow, I notice Ivy – who lives across the road from Elvis – is pouring Tequila into shot glasses.

When I ask what the shots are for, she looks at me blankly and then says they are for the *Extreme Bingo* that they're going to play after the game of Twister has finished.

Apparently, *Extreme Bingo* involves watching old episodes of Gardeners' World and taking a shot every time Monty Don says: 'very erect with a lovely purple head', 'prune your cherry' and 'lots of bushy side growth'.

Ivy says the last time they all played *Extreme Bingo*, Monty was making a Tit box and they all woke up three days later.

TUESDAY 17ᵀᴴ AUGUST

Back to the houses on the dunes.

Uncle Dave isn't cutting Mrs Taylor's grass anymore. He says it's because Gaz is there every day, painting the fence a different colour and 'he can cut the bloody grass himself, if that effing overgrown sheep can't keep the lawn down'. But I'm fairly certain it's because whenever we see Mrs Taylor on her way to the beach or the village shop, she blows Uncle Dave a kiss and gives a little boob jiggle.

Luckily, the dog shit I mowed around at the holiday house last time has melted in the rain, so normal service resumes.

I cut the sodding new garden, with the ankle-twisting front lawn and cherub-spitting water feature and Uncle Dave smirks when he comes back to pick up me and my mower. I think I might go on strike if I have to cut this one again.

Uncle Dave parks on the double yellow lines outside the butcher's shop so I can nip in and get us both a pie for lunch, and then spends the rest of our lunch break arguing with the Traffic Warden.

Uncle Dave says there should be special allowances made if you're an effing local, because it's the effing locals who keep this effing community afloat once all the effing visitors have gone effing home.

The traffic warden doesn't seem to be listening and just points at the double yellow lines and asks if Uncle Dave is colour blind. Uncle Dave says that the traffic warden is nothing more than an effing-wannabe-policeman and if he'd effing studied harder at effing school, he could have had an effing proper effing job. The Traffic Warden then asked what a proper job was? Like a Gardener, or something? And Uncle Dave revved the van's engine really loudly and said that at least Dick Turpin had worn an effing mask when he was effing robbing people.

After my chicken and mushroom pie, I cut two lawns in Aidan Drive and Uncle Dave tries to ignore Mrs Taylor, who is sunbathing in a bikini with Mrs Wilson at Number Six.

THURSDAY 19TH AUGUST

Turns out poor Mrs Higginsbottom is in hospital.

The Major said she had driven to the village shop yesterday afternoon for a twelve pack of Wotsits, a Yorkie, a Fry's Turkish Delight, and a four pack of Wispa, and she crashed into the lamp post at the corner of the village green on her way home.

Someone called an ambulance but then there was a massive panic because Mrs Higginsbottom wasn't in her car and couldn't be found anywhere. Then someone who was on holiday, tripped over while they were making a TikTok, and discovered they had fallen over Mrs Higginsbottom, who was attempting to crawl home with her bag for life clasped between her teeth.

Anyway, she had a nasty cut on her forehead because she wasn't wearing her seatbelt, and the hospital wanted to keep her in overnight for observation.

Mrs Higginsbottom called Elvis last night and demanded that Elvis use the spare key to her house, to get some of her cake and bring it to the hospital. Elvis asked if she needed a change of clothes, but Mrs Higginsbottom just replied that she needed cake because you're not allowed to smoke in a hospital.

I didn't even know Mrs Higginsbottom smoked! These old people really are dark horses.

TUESDAY 24TH AUGUST

Rubbish weather.

It rained at six o' clock this morning and I'm unclogging the mower and emptying the catcher like a one-armed-juggler on crystal meth. Uncle Dave says because the sun is out, the grass will dry quickly, but I still have a lie down in the back of the van at lunchtime because I'm knackered.

While I'm settling down for my nanna nap, Uncle Dave announces he's going to the Frog for a quick pint. When I say I thought he was barred from the Frog, he lights a Lambert & Butler and admits that Brian rang him last night and un-barred him. Uncle Dave says Brian said there was a chance that the brewery would refuse to deliver his order on Monday, as the Frog had suffered such a drop in wet sales recently.

Uncle Dave returns to Aidan Drive smelling like a micro-brewery at quarter to five.

It feels like I've cut eight hectares of grass while he's been on his unplanned afternoon off, so I go on strike and refuse to do Number Twenty-Four with the raised beds on the back lawn.

While I sit on the kerb in the sun, Uncle Dave can be heard crashing around the garden, and there's a small fire when he puts his Lambert & Butler on the ground while he's re-filling the mower's petrol tank.

THURSDAY 26ᵀᴴ AUGUST

It was Uncle Dave's birthday yesterday and he didn't get home until three o' clock this morning.

Brian was so pleased with how much cash was coming over the bar at the Frog from Uncle Dave and his pals, he locked the door and let them continue after closing time. Apparently, there was one dicey moment when Karl, the local Copper, hammered on the door at two-thirty-seven and told them to keep the bloody noise down. Brian assured him that everyone in the bar was a resident at the pub, and the bar was licenced to stay open for residents.

I think this would have been OK until Uncle Dave shouted: 'Is that effing twelve-year-old Bobby trying to spoil our effing fun? Why is he not at home studying for his effing GCSEs?!' and Brian was forced to chuck them out.

It mustn't have ended that badly though, because Uncle Brian got a lift home in the panda car but was really annoyed that Karl wouldn't turn on the blues and twos even though it was his birthday.

At first, when we start on Aidan Drive, I think Uncle Dave amazingly hasn't got a hangover, until he hops in the van and goes to the baker's shop and returns with a heart attack in a roll. He shovels in the bacon, sausage, black pudding, egg, and beans, before retreating for a lie down in the back of the van, while I discover that someone has staked that bloody Weeping Willow and it's now upright again.

Make a note on my phone reminding me to buy more copper nails.

TUESDAY 31ST AUGUST

Start at Aidan Drive and notice that Number Twenty-Four, where I've previously managed to shred a Hoster, some Lady's Mantle, and destroy their sprinkler system, hose, and collection of ceramic pots, have installed chicken wire and garden cane fencing around most of their shrubs and raised beds. There's still a big, scorched mark on the grass from Uncle Dave's fire last week, and I manage to run the mower over three empty plastic flowerpots beside the compost bin and realign the barbeque they have made out of bricks. Feel slightly bad when a white-haired bloke comes out of the house and offers me a slice of pizza and a glass of Dr Pepper. I down the Dr Pepper and start eating the pizza while I'm pushing the mower down to Number Twenty. I discover what I assumed were pieces of red pepper on the pizza are actually chillies, and they are so hot my tongue and lips are numb. Bloody git. Make a note on my phone to draw a huge cock and balls on his lawn in weedkiller on my last day.

THURSDAY 2ND SEPTEMBER

Back to the houses on the dunes, which are a quick job as the growth rate of the grass is slowing down due to the sandy soil. (My God, I'm an expert on grass these days.) Then it's the holiday house that I need crampons for, and then on to the Major's. He's not in but has left me a bottle of Marston's Pedigree which after drinking it, I'm seeing two mowers in front of me. Mrs Higginsbottom claps her hands in amusement when I tell her I drank the whole bottle of Pedigree, and she offers me a pick-me-up in the form of a glass of orange juice. It tastes fine, but when I'm pushing the mower next door to Elvis's house, I see a huge tiger, like the size of a car, run in front of me and the sky looks like the sun is setting even though it's half-past-three. When I do Elvis's lawn, I keep thinking the mower is a giant cabbage that I need to push really slowly in case it unravels.

Uncle Dave has been to do the holiday house that's outside the village and I'm feeling a bit more normal by the time he comes to pick me up.

Mrs Taylor is sunbathing in a bikini on the bench opposite Elvis's house. She gives Uncle Dave a wave, but he ignores her and lights a Lambert & Butler as I wrestle my mower into the back of the van.

We stop at the Frog for a quick pint, which turns into nine pints, eleven whisky chasers and two jugs of Fruity Loopy. Barry-the-Builder comes in at half-past-nine and says he's taking his missus to London at the weekend to see *The Lion King*. Uncle Dave says he's never seen a musical in his life, and Barry says the only musical Uncle Dave should see is *Joseph and the Amazing Technicolour Dreamgoat*.

Get chucked out after Uncle Dave threatens to punch Barry and Brian sings: 'I've been through the desert on a goat with no name' as he pushes me and Uncle Dave out the door.

TUESDAY 7TH SEPTEMBER

My last week grass cutting because college starts next Monday.

Uncle Dave asks if I would prefer to be a gardener instead of studying Tourism and Hospitality at Newcastle College. He says it like I'm going to college to study TikTok. But I have to admit, I'm tanned and have stomach muscles that would rival an Olympic sprinter. Shame grass doesn't grow all year round really.

We start at Aidan Drive, and I see the Weeping willow has broken away from its stake. I jump up and down on it a few times to try and encourage it to give up the will to live.

As it's my last week, Uncle Dave offers to go and buy us lunch. I again suggest a lobster roll from the place down the road, but he returns with a tepid toastie from the pub and a packet of Bacon Frazzles. Still, it's an improvement on a cold scotch pie from the Co-Op.

Uncle Dave shoots off to do a couple of lawns down on the dunes, leaving me with Ebba Road. The git. He'll be parked up, reading the *Daily Star* by the time I've done the Major's. Decide to eat and drink whatever is offered to me on Ebba Road. When Uncle Dave returns in the van three hours later, I've put away a bottle of Old Peculiar at the Major's, three slices of cake and half a bottle of Harvey's Bristol Cream at Mrs Higginsbottom's and two packets of cheese and onion crisps, a packet of mini cheddars, seventeen Werther's Originals, a sausage roll, a packet of Cadbury's chocolate buttons, a white chocolate Magnum, a tub of Ben & Jerry's cookie dough ice cream and a can of Coke at Elvis's house.

Can't remember being taken home.

THURSDAY 9TH SEPTEMBER

It's my last day!

I'm a bit sad really, because I like the Major, Mrs Higginsbottom, and Elvis, and I want to make sure the old couple on the dunes with the enormous underwear are OK.

Me and Uncle Dave mow the ones on the dunes that he didn't do the other day and then there's two to do in Aidan Drive. After that Uncle Dave goes to do the one outside the village, leaving me with the ankle-breaking front lawn of St James' Park with the dodgy water-vomiting cherubs. Turns out the owner of the house is in residence and, after she has looked at me as though I am a beggar scrounging money for drugs, she asks me if I do anything more than cutting the grass. The sweat is rolling down my forehead after battling with the forty-five-degree lawn and I know my face looks like I have been lying on a beach in Spain for seven hours with no sunscreen. But I flash her a smile, and advise her that I'm definitely straight, and anything other than grass cutting is f**king well and truly off the cards.

Walk away dragging my mower as she shouts, 'I meant weeding!'

Find I don't really care.

Uncle Dave suggests I go and say hello to the Major, Mrs Higginsbottom and Elvis, as it's my last day, and he will go and buy lunch. Tell him if it's not a lobster roll, I'm going to slash his van tyres and pour sugar into the tanks of both mowers. He mutters something under his breath as he goes to his van, and I go to Elvis's house.

Turns out, the Major, Mrs Higginsbottom and Elvis, wanted to throw me a quick surprise lunch of lobster rolls, cake and sherry. I avoid the cake, but tuck into

36

lobster with lemon mayonnaise and my schooner glass is just being topped up with Croft Original, when Uncle Dave turns up with a Greggs vegan sausage roll.

The Major tells Uncle Dave that 'no buggar on earth should be eating a vegan sausage roll for lunch,' and Mrs Higginsbottom adds that 'they should always be served for supper with a nice dollop of piccalilli and some caramelised onion chutney.'

Uncle Dave has a slice of chocolate cake, two vanilla cupcakes, a piece of carrot cake, and an almond slice.

I drive him home, as he eats his way through a big bag of Doritos, two DairyLea Ham and Cheese Lunchables and a box of Mr Kipling's Cherry Bakewells.

MONDAY 13TH SEPTEMBER – FIRST DAY AT COLLEGE

I'm wide awake seventeen minutes before my alarm goes off.

Mum is taking me to the train and she's sitting at the table, holding a cup of tea when I walk into the kitchen.

There's a card wishing me luck from Elvis, Mrs Higginsbottom and the Major. There's also a Tupperware box full of traybakes, with a note encouraging me to take them with me and share them with my new friends.

I leave the lid on the box firmly closed but when Dad picks me up from the station that night, his eyes are kind of glazed and he's playing Elvis's songs on Spotify.

Instead of going straight home, we go to the Macdonald's drive-thru and he orders a cheeseburger for me, and a Twenty Chicken McNuggets Sharebox, a Filet-o-Fish, large fries, a quarter pounder with cheese, a McChicken Sandwich, a banana shake, a Coke, and a McFlurry for himself.

I didn't even think he liked Macdonald's.

Dad drops me at the Happy Frog for a quick pint, but Uncle Dave and Barry-the-Builder are there, and the quick pint turns into seven pints, four whisky chasers, two jugs of Funny Bunny, and three of the new cocktails that Brian has on the menu called *Float the Goat*.

Gaz is behind the bar and he looks ill. His face is white, he's sweating, and he twice gives Uncle Dave the wrong change. Barry says it's because Mrs Taylor's hot tub arrived this morning and while Gaz was setting it up with the chemicals and everything, Mrs Taylor was leaning against the patio door, swinging the cord of her silk dressing gown suggestively. I ask Gaz if he's working for Mrs Taylor tomorrow and he starts to shake, takes a measure of vodka from the optic and swigs it down in one go. He says he's tried to tell Mrs Taylor that he has lots of shifts at the Happy Frog and he doesn't really have time to be painting the fence yet another colour, but she just laughed and suggested that he took off his t-shirt as it's so hot. Barry says that Gaz should grow a pair and tell her where to get off and when Uncle Dave agrees, Barry says that maybe Uncle Dave should have told the goat where to get off when it was eating his jeans. Uncle Dave says he's going to effing punch Barry if he mentions the effing goat again and Barry just laughs and asks Gaz what colour the fence in Mrs Taylor's garden is now. Gaz says Mrs Taylor is now happy with the fence being battle-ship grey and his next job is to build a shed for Martha the goat to sleep in for the winter. Uncle Dave and Barry start singing 'Build a little goathouse in your soul' and Gaz threatens to bar them both.

When Dad comes to pick me up, he's halfway down a tub of Mini Heroes that he found in the cupboard under the stairs. As I fasten my seatbelt, we watch Uncle Dave and Barry-the-Builder singing the Madness song 'Our House' as Gaz forcibly evicts them from the Frog. It's just as Dad is driving past them that I realise that they are substituting the word 'goat' for 'house.'

Arrive home with a lap full of mini hero wrappers and a fear that the Frog will die a death if both Uncle Dave and Barry-the-builder are barred.

TUESDAY 4TH JANUARY - UPDATE

I can't believe it! There was a massive Police raid in Cresthill last night.

I got a WhatsApp from my friend Carrie when I was on the train to college this morning, saying that the Police thought there was something suspicious about a garden not having any frost on it, when the neighbouring gardens were completely white after the snow last night.

Then I get another message (a text for Christ's sake because Uncle Dave hasn't got to grips with WhatsApp yet), and Uncle Dave says the Rozzers were at Mrs Higginsbottom's because the massive heaters she was using to keep her greenhouse plants alive had thawed all the snow off the roof of the greenhouse, and the lawn, and off the back of the house as well.

Anyway, both the Major and Elvis, who was wearing her/his/Elvis's best white suit and penny loafers, both told the police that the plants in Mrs Higginsbottom's greenhouse had been there for literally years, like long before Mrs Higginsbottom bought the house twenty-two years ago. And they all thought they were some kind of *exotic* plants because the previous owner of the house had been a Botanist, who had once been stranded on Mars for months and cultivated his own potatoes, and the police had simply sent in a team who pulled up all the exotic plants, put them in bin bags and took them away.

Uncle Dave said Mrs Higginsbottom wasn't that bothered about the exotic plants in her greenhouse because it was costing her a fortune to heat it, to keep the plants alive. But as she has another thirty-seven of the exotic plants in her loft, all was not lost.

I'll never understand gardeners. The lengths they go to,

to keep plants alive is stupid.

Uncle Dave then said if I want to help him cut grass in my college holidays, he could use the help. He said it in a gruff way, as if he's not bothered; but I know he is. And I'm actually quite flattered.

Jeff, a bloke from Cresthill, helped Uncle Dave cut grass a couple of summers ago and Uncle Dave said he wouldn't ask him to help him again. In fact, when I think about it, Uncle Dave told me in the Happy Frog one night that Jeff was about as useful as an effing ashtray on an effing motorbike. Jeff was just coming back from the gents at the time and replied that if Uncle Dave had effing brains, he would be effing dangerous. Then Brian said that Jeff was so thick he made Katie Price look like a Futures and Options Trader, and Jeff asked if this Katie Price worked in the Tourist Information shop, and Brian just laughed and told him to keep talking, so they could record it, in case he said something clever.

I haven't told Uncle Dave that Brian has offered me a holiday job in the Happy Frog, which would fit in with my course and give me some relevant work experience. And I should take it, I know I should.

Thing is, it pays more to cut grass. So, maybe I will take Uncle Dave up on his offer.

Just for one more summer.

And I won't eat any cake.

ABOUT THE AUTHOR

Helen lives in Northumberland with her husband and daughter. They are accompanied by a rabbit called Neville, a useless cat and a horse who has a strenuous aversion to the Vet.
You can follow Helen on social media, visit her website for more details.

www.helennewmanwood.com

Printed in Great Britain
by Amazon

43308853R00030